MR. FUNNY

by Roger Hargreaves

EGMONT

Mr Funny lived in a teapot!

It had two bedrooms, a bathroom, a kitchen and a living room, and it suited Mr Funny very nicely.

One day, Mr Funny was having lunch.

He wasn't very hungry, so he only had a daisy sandwich and a glass of toast!

"Delicious," he murmured to himself as he finished his funny lunch.

After lunch, Mr Funny decided to go for a drive in his car.

Mr Funny's car was a shoe!

Have you ever seen a car that looks like a shoe?

It looks very funny!

As he drove along, everybody who saw him laughed to see such a funny sight.

He passed a worm at the side of the road.

The worm thought Mr Funny in his funny car was the funniest thing he had ever seen.

He nearly laughed himself in two!

He passed a pig in a field.

The pig thought Mr Funny in his funny car was the funniest thing she had ever seen.

She nearly laughed her tail off!

Even the flowers he passed thought that Mr Funny was the funniest thing they had ever seen.

They nearly laughed themselves out of the ground!

Eventually, Mr Funny came to some crossroads.

He didn't know which way to go, so he looked at the signpost.

One of the signs said TO THE ZOO.

"That will be fun," thought Mr Funny to himself, so he drove his shoe towards the zoo.

When he arrived at the gate of the zoo, he stopped.

It was closed.

"I'm sorry," said the zoo keeper. "We've had to close the zoo because all the animals have colds, and they're all feeling very sorry for themselves."

"Oh dear," said Mr Funny, and then he thought. "Perhaps I can help to cheer them up," he said.

"Well," said the zoo keeper, "it's worth a try." And he opened the gate.

Mr Funny drove into the zoo.

In his shoe.

The first thing he saw was an elephant. It was true.
The elephant was feeling very sorry for herself.
Very sorry indeed.

Mr Funny stood and looked at the sad-looking
elephant.

And the sad-looking elephant stood and looked at
Mr Funny.

Oh dear!

Then, do you know what Mr Funny did?

He pulled a funny face!

Mr Funny, as you'd imagine, is very good at pulling funny faces.

The elephant giggled.

She'd never seen anything so funny.

Mr Funny pulled another funny face.

The elephant burst out laughing.

The elephant laughed and laughed and laughed.

She laughed so hard, she nearly laughed her trunk off!

And she felt a lot lot better.

Mr Funny went over to the lion house.

There was a lion, feeling extraordinarily sorry for himself.

Mr Funny stood and looked at the sad-looking lion.

And the sad-looking lion stood and looked at Mr Funny.

Oh dear!

And then Mr Funny pulled the funniest-looking face that's probably ever been pulled anywhere, ever.

Now, you've heard a lion roar before, haven't you?

Well, this lion roared too – with laughter.

He laughed so hard he nearly laughed his whiskers to pieces.

Then Mr Funny went around to see all the other animals in the zoo.

Oh dear, what a miserable-looking lot!

For all of them, Mr Funny pulled funnier and funnier faces.

The big brown bear giggled, and then burst out laughing.

And the giraffe laughed so hard she nearly laughed her neck into a knot. And the hippopotamus nearly laughed himself out of his skin. And the penguins nearly laughed their flippers floppy. And the leopard, well, you really should have seen him, he laughed so hard he nearly laughed his spots off!

What pandemonium!

"Oh, Mr Funny," giggled the zoo keeper, who had started laughing as well. "Oh, Mr Funny, thank you very very much indeed for coming to cheer us all up!"

"Oh, it was nothing really," replied Mr Funny modestly, and drove off.

In his shoe!

Later, when Mr Funny arrived home, he chuckled to himself. "Well," he said, "that's the end of another funny day!"

And he parked his shoe and went inside his teapot and, because he was feeling thirsty, he made himself
…

… a nice hot cup of cake!